Aimee Carson

Cómo romper un corazón

Editado por HARLEQUIN IBÉRICA, S.A.
Núñez de Balboa, 56
28001 Madrid

I.S.B.N.: 978-84-687-2398-3
Depósito legal: M-35514-2012
Editor responsable: Luis Pugni
Fotomecánica: M.T. Color & Diseño, S.L. Las Rozas (Madrid)
Impresión en Black print CPI (Barcelona)
Fecha impresion para Argentina: 1.7.13
Distribuidor exclusivo para España: LOGISTA
Distribuidor para México: CODIPLYRSA
Distribuidores para Argentina: interior, BERTRAN, S.A.C. Vélez
Sársfield, 1950. Cap. Fed./ Buenos Aires y Gran Buenos Aires,
VACCARO SÁNCHEZ y Cía, S.A.

BORN AGAIN

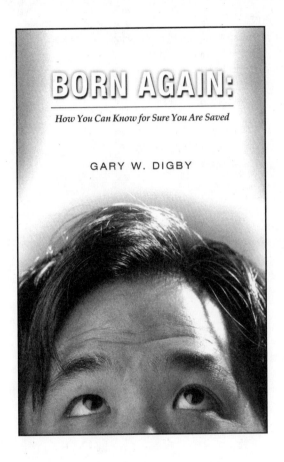

BORN AGAIN:

How You Can Know for Sure You Are Saved

GARY W. DIGBY

HighWay

A division of Anomalos Publishing House

HighWay
A division of Anomalos Publishing House, Crane 65633
© 2009 by Dr. Gary W. Digby
1909 Merlin Drive
Jefferson City, MO 65101
garydigby@aol.com

All rights reserved. Published 2009
Printed in the United States of America

09   1

ISBN-10: 0982036175 (paper)
EAN- 13: 9780982036174 (paper)

A CIP catalog record for this book is available from the Library of
Congress.

Cover illustration and design by Steve Warner

Unless otherwise noted, scripture references are from the New
King James Version.

CONTENTS

PREFACE

You have professed faith in Jesus Christ as your personal Lord and Savior. You have been baptized and have become part of a Bible-believing, evangelical church. Yet, sometimes, within the deepest recesses of your heart, there is an uneasy feeling, even fear, that you have never truly been saved.

If this describes you, then you are not alone. Unfortunately, after more than thirty years in vocational ministry, I have discovered this is a common problem. Some who live with doubt keep it a secret, hoping the doubts will go away, and no one will ever know. Others, searching for an answer to their dilemma, confide in their pastor, a friend, or a family member.

One lady who went through this experience for several years, shared with me that she would actually awaken her husband in the middle of the night demanding, "Are you sure you are saved? How can you know for sure?" Her husband, annoyed, would reply, "Yes, I am sure! Now please, go back to sleep!"

Rest assured, it is not God's desire for people to live in constant fear that they are not saved. "There is no fear in love; but perfect love casts out fear, because fear involves torment" (1 John 4:18). The love to which this verse refers is not our love, but God's love, which we receive in our hearts when God saves us. Living with fear and uncertainty is not part of the abundant life Jesus came to give those who believe in him.

I wrote this book to provide helpful insight and instruction to those who are living with doubt or who have family and friends who are experiencing this problem. It was also written for those who have young children and sense the need for greater insight and understanding in preparing to counsel them effectively concerning coming to faith in Christ.

In the chapters that follow, we will consider how God's Spirit works in our hearts, enabling us to come to Christ in saving faith. We will examine what it means to believe in Jesus Christ—what saving faith is and what saving faith is not. Lastly, we will review scripture that helps us determine if we are truly in the faith—if we have actually been born again. God's word tells us that we can know for sure we are saved, "I write these things to you who believe in the name of the Son of God that you may know that you have eternal life" (1 John 5:13, NIV).

As you continue reading, I trust you will do so with an open mind, an open heart, and an open Bible. Rather than doubt, may God fill your heart with peace and assurance that your sins are forgiven and that you have been saved by his amazing grace.

A SPECIAL NOTE TO READERS

In the pages of this book, you will read personal accounts of people coming to know Jesus Christ as Savior and Lord. These true stories give testimony to the reality of knowing him. It is hoped that the story-telling approach will make the subject interesting and readable while at the same time imparting vital information. However, this approach provides an opening for a particular criticism sometimes voiced concerning personal testimonies, which is "you seem to think that a person is not really saved unless a great emotional feeling is experienced." If you are inclined to agree with this sentiment and therefore not read this book, I ask you to pause and consider that the book does present specific indicators for testing the reality of our salvation. Moreover, emotional experience is not one of these indicators. However, also consider that salvation does include forgiveness of sin and new life in Christ, which makes for enduring joy and peace. So, experience it we must, if our salvation is real. We just need to make sure that we test our experience in light of Biblical truth. I challenge you not to put this book aside. Instead, use it along with every other available resource until you know for sure you are saved.

ACKNOWLEDGMENTS

As with any project, this book would not have been completed without the assistance of many people. I am grateful to all of them, including those whose experiences make up the heart of the book.

I am also deeply appreciative to my wife, Annette, for her constant encouragement and for doing the initial word processing of the manuscript;

To our son and daughter, Jeremy and Christy, and to my brother, Charles, for their attention to detail while proofreading the manuscript and their helpful suggestions throughout the process;

To my brother, Lloyd, a special thanks for his insightful counsel, thought-provoking questions, constant feedback, and many hours of editorial assistance on every version of the manuscript.

Finally, I would like to acknowledge the editorial assistance and overall support from everyone at Anomalos Publishing who worked with me on this project and whose positive attitude sustained me throughout the process.

THE HOLY SPIRIT REVEALS

OUR GREAT NEED

CHAPTER ONE

'Twas grace that taught my heart to fear
And grace my fears relieved;
How precious did that grace appear,
The hour I first believed.

— Newton, 1779

A VALUED HERITAGE

Having been born on a small hill farm in northeast Mississippi, Walter had always been accustomed to hard work, never having known anything else. On this beautiful summer morning though, something was wrong. As he cultivated a field of corn with a mule and single-stock plow, his thoughts were deeply troubled.

The annual revival meeting at Mt. Pleasant Baptist Church, the family's home church, had recently begun. During that meeting, the Holy Spirit had begun dealing with Walter's heart, convicting him that he was lost and needed to be saved. His experience was similar to that of the man described in the classic metaphorical book by John Bunyan (1928) entitled *The Pilgrim's Progress*. Bunyan wrote: "I saw a man clothed with rags standing in a certain place, with his face from his own house, a book in his hand, and a great burden upon his back. I looked, and saw him open the book, and read therein; and as he read, he wept and trembled; and not being able longer to contain, he broke out with a lamentable cry, saying, 'What shall I do?'" (p. 11).

Walter too had become keenly aware of the warnings from the book, and he knew he stood condemned before God.

For several days, he had earnestly sought the Lord for the forgiveness of his sins but to no avail. More than once, when the altar call was given during the meeting, he had gone forward to the mourner's bench for prayer and counsel. Still, he was unable to find relief from the burden that weighed so heavily upon his heart. As Walter pondered these thoughts in his mind, he reached the end of another cornrow. Hollering at his mule to whoa, he turned the plow stock over on its side and hurried into the woods, determined to stay there until he knew his sins had been forgiven and that he had been saved by God's grace.

Later that morning, one of Walter's younger brothers, Hollis, who was not yet old enough to work in the fields, was in the front yard playing. Years later, Hollis would recall how, all of a sudden, he heard someone yelling and immediately thought something bad must have happened. He looked up the little dirt road that ran in front of the home place and saw that it was Walter. Hollis called for his mother to come quickly. She came dashing out of the house onto the front porch. By that time, Walter had made it to the front yard. Anxiously, his mother demanded, "Walter, what's wrong with you?" Walter's simple reply was, "Ma, I've made my peace with God." Shortly afterward, Walter publicly professed his faith in Christ, and he was baptized at Mt. Pleasant Baptist Church. The rest of his life, until he died at the age of seventy-eight, Walter loved to tell the story of how the Lord saved his soul as a teenage boy on that wooded hillside so many years before.

While growing up, this was just one of many testimonies I heard that influenced me in a meaningful way. Testimonies such as this from relatives and from other people made a wonderful and lasting impression upon my young mind. You see, the little boy in the front yard, Hollis, was my father, and Walter was his oldest brother. Of course, their mother was my grandmother. All three are now with the Lord in heaven.

SOMEWHAT PERSONAL

Very seldom does one hear testimonies such as Uncle Walter's anymore. In fact, such testimonies are sometimes discouraged or frowned upon. Some would argue there is a danger of potentially influencing people to place their confidence in emotion, rather than placing it in God's word. I would suggest, however, that such testimonies could serve a very useful purpose. In my own experience, hearing how God worked in other people's lives to awaken them to their true spiritual condition and bring them to a saving knowledge of Jesus Christ was both instructive and encouraging. I too wanted to know this Savior and to know my sins were forgiven.

My spiritual journey was also impacted by the fact that I was blessed to have been born into a strong Christian family. My mother and father came to know the Lord years before I was ever born and were deeply committed believers. We were present at Sunday school and church each week. In addition, God was an ever-present reality in our home. He was not just someone to whom we paid tribute on Sunday and then forgot about the rest of the week. My brothers and I learned that God was real, and he was the center of our parents' lives. We witnessed the love and reverence our parents had for the Lord and their dependence upon him for provision and protection every day.

One of the things I learned at an early age was that to become a Christian, a person must repent of sin and trust Jesus Christ as his or her Lord and Savior. From my parents, as well as through Sunday school and church, I learned that Jesus Christ is the Son of God, that he was born of a virgin, that he lived a sinless life, that he died on the cross to pay my sin debt, that he rose again the third day, and that he ascended back to the Father. All of this, I knew as far back as I could remember and never doubted it was all true. At about ten years of age, though, the fact that I was a sinner and needed a Savior took on a new and different dimension. At that time in my life, this truth became more than just words, more than just impersonal information. It became a living reality of which I was consciously aware most of the time.

Before, I had known intellectually that I was a sinner and needed to be saved, but when the Holy Spirit brought conviction upon my heart, this truth became personal and experiential in nature. What made the situation even worse for me was that everyone else in our family, my parents and two brothers, had already been saved. If I died or if Jesus came again, I knew that I would be the only one in my family who was not prepared to meet Jesus. Dread and fear filled my heart. Even though I knew the plan of salvation mentally, I also knew that mere mental assent was not enough. To join the church and to be baptized without having truly been saved would have only made matters worse. As Jesus informed Nicodemus, I knew that I must be born again. I prayed and sought the Lord but could not find the peace I so desperately sought. This dilemma continued for what, to me, seemed like an eternity. I had begun to wonder if I would ever be saved. Perhaps I was destined to be lost forever.

One Tuesday night in April 1964, our family returned home from an evangelistic service at our church. Everyone went to bed and went to sleep, everyone except me.

Instead, I was earnestly praying. Having reached a point of utter hopelessness, I felt that I just had to get this settled, that I had to know that I was saved and I would go to be with Jesus if I died. In the darkness and silence of the night, I prayed with all my heart, "Dear Lord, I know I am a sinner. I am lost and if I were to die, I know I would spend eternity in hell. Lord, I know that you died on the cross for me and that you rose again the third day. Lord, I want to be saved, and I need to be saved, but I don't know *how* to be saved. I don't know *how* to repent, and I don't know *how* to believe. If I did, I would. Lord, I can't figure this out and if I am ever going to be saved, you will simply have to do it."

At that moment in time, I knew that I was shut up to God, shut up to his mercy and his grace. There was no other source of hope and if God were to choose not to help me, I knew I would be lost forever. That my soul and eternal fate lay completely in his hands became transparently clear to me. It was all up to him. I could do nothing but cast myself upon him. It was at that moment, the burden of my heart rolled away, and I knew my sins were forgiven. Peace and joy replaced conviction and condemnation, as Jesus became precious to my heart.

A few years later, when reading the testimony of Charles Haddon Spurgeon, I was able to identify with his experience in several ways. Since he lived with his grandfather who was a preacher, he learned much about the Bible and the gospel at an early age. When Spurgeon was in his teens, the Holy Spirit awakened him to his lost condition. He prayed and earnestly sought the Lord but became discouraged and just about lost hope because he could find no relief for his troubled soul.

Then, one bitterly cold Sunday morning, as Spurgeon was walking down a snow-covered street, he saw a little Methodist church and decided to go in. Because of the winter's blizzard, the pastor was absent that day. Instead, an untrained and inexperienced layman spoke in his place. For his text, he used Isaiah 45:22 (KJV), "Look unto me, and be ye saved, All ye ends of the earth, for I am God, and there is none else."

As the speaker explained the meaning of his text, he stressed that the only thing the people in the wilderness could do to escape death from the serpents' bites was to look by faith at the serpent made of brass affixed by Moses on a pole. He then explained that a person could only be saved from sin and its penalty by looking to Jesus through eyes of faith and beholding his dying upon the cross, paying our sin debt. He emphasized that a look of faith is all that is required to be delivered from the sentence of death.

As he contemplated these words, Spurgeon saw and understood for the first time that all he had to do was look; indeed, all he *could* do was look. As he, by faith, looked upon Jesus dying in his place, he was saved. The peace and assurance young Spurgeon had sought for so long now filled his soul.

In his autobiography, Spurgeon (2007) shed greater light upon his conversion experience when he wrote:

> I had heard of the plan of salvation by the sacrifice of Jesus from my youth up; but I did not know any more about it in my innermost soul than if I had been born and bred a Hottentot [note: the thought being of someone who had never heard the gospel and knew nothing about the God of the Bible]. The light was there, but I was blind; it was of necessity that the Lord Himself should make the matter plain to me...When...I received

the gospel to my soul's salvation, I thought that I had never really heard it before…But, on looking back, I am inclined to believe that I had heard the gospel fully preached many hundreds of times before…and when I did hear it, the message may not have been any more clear in itself than it had been at former times, but the power of the Holy Spirit was present to open my ear, and to guide the message to my heart. (p. 98)

Even though Spurgeon had understood the gospel intellectually, and had earnestly sought salvation, he was not able to believe unto the saving of his soul until the Holy Spirit enabled him to understand the gospel with a clarity and perception he had never known before.

In *The Pilgrim's Progress*, John Bunyan gave a similarly wonderful description of Christian finding deliverance from the burden that weighed him down.

Up this way therefore did burdened Christian run, but not without great difficulty, because of the load on his back. He thus ran till he came at a place somewhat ascending; and upon that place stood a cross, and a little below, in the bottom, a sepulcher. So I saw in my dream, that just as Christian came up with the cross, his burden loosed from off his shoulders, and fell from off his back, and began to tumble, and so continued to do till it came to the mouth of the sepulcher, where it fell in, and I saw it no more. (pp. 55–56)

After his own conversion to Christ, Spurgeon (1899) commented on the effect it had on him when he read about Christian's conversion as described in *The Pilgrim's Progress*. Spurgeon wrote: "I felt so interested in the poor fellow [Christian] that I thought I should jump with joy when, after he had carried his heavy load so long, he at last got rid of it; and that was how I felt when the burden of guilt, which I had borne so long, was forever rolled from my shoulders and my heart" (p. 103). It was at the cross where Christian's burden fell away, and he saw it no more.

In his letter to the church at Rome, the Apostle Paul wrote this concerning the peace we enjoy when we come to faith in Christ, "Therefore, having been justified by faith,

we have peace with God through our Lord Jesus Christ"
(Rom. 5:1). The verb used in the Greek text is the word
dikaiothentes, which means, "having been justified." This verb
is a participle (considered a verb in Greek) in the aorist
tense, meaning that this justification occurred at a particular point in time (aorist tense denotes punctilious action,
not durative action). That "point in time" was the moment
they believed or, as Paul later wrote in this same letter,
the moment they "...believed unto righteousness" (Rom.
10:10). The main verb used in Romans 5:1 is the word *exo-
men* and is translated "we have" in which Paul states, "...we
have peace with God." He was explaining to his readers
that they were experiencing peace with God because God
had already justified them, which means God judicially and
legally had declared them righteous. When did God justify
them? The moment they believed. On what basis was God
able to justify them? On the basis that Jesus Christ died for
them on the cross, paying their sin-debt, and triumphantly
rose again from the dead.

As the Apostle Paul explained in scripture and as
Christian, Spurgeon, and Uncle Walter experienced, I too
experienced peace with God through our Lord Jesus Christ

on that Tuesday evening in April 1964. Now, I could joyfully proclaim with the songwriter:

> *At the cross, at the cross, where I first saw the light,*
> *And the burden of my heart, rolled away;*
> *It was there by faith, I received my sight*
> *And, now I am happy all the day.*
>
> —Hudson, "At the Cross"

REFLECTIONS ON CHAPTER 1

1. The Holy Spirit works in people's hearts to make them aware of their great need of salvation.
2. Salvation is a work of grace done by God himself.
3. Peace and joy replace guilt and condemnation when a person is saved by God's grace.

CAN YOU KNOW FOR SURE?

The Spirit Himself bears witness with
our spirit that we are children of God.

— R o m a n s   8 : 1 6

A TROUBLING SITUATION

"Instead of our regular Bible study, this morning we are going to do something different. All classes will meet together, and everyone who desires to will have an opportunity to share your personal testimony of how you came to faith in Christ," said the director of the Youth Sunday School Department. This was a fitting way to prepare the youth for the church's evangelistic campaign that began that Sunday morning and extended through Friday evening.

Many people in the twenty-first century may not be familiar with weeklong evangelistic campaigns, commonly referred to as "revivals." A revival typically included a guest speaker preaching evangelistic messages and often included personal testimonies by those who were already saved as the church focused on reaching the community with the gospel. The practice of Christians sharing about how they came to faith in Christ during worship services or group meetings may seem unusual and even threatening today. But, this was common practice not too many years ago as people looked forward to sharing what the Lord had done for them.

Annette (my wife) and I taught in this youth department. We, along with almost everyone present that morning, shared how we came to faith in Jesus Christ. We were surprised and somewhat perplexed, however, because many who shared admitted not knowing for sure when they were saved. They were often plagued with doubt as to whether or not they had actually been saved. Several in the group had been baptized two or three times and still were not sure about their salvation. Several concluded their comments with "I feel that I am saved at this point in time, even though I have often dealt with doubts." Not only was this testimony of living with doubt given by many students, but also by several teachers.

This was something different and puzzling to Annette and me. We needed to process what we had heard because both of us knew when we were saved and knew Christ lived in our hearts. We could not understand how so many young people and adults, most of whom had grown up in church, could have so much uncertainty about whether or not they were saved and whether or not they were going to heaven when they died. What made the situation even more perplexing was that this was a Bible-believing, Bible-preaching church. We were familiar with people experiencing doubt about their salvation, but this was different in that the majority of the people in this Sunday school department seemed to have serious doubts about their salvation, could not go back to a time when they met the Lord, and seemed to be living a life characterized by uncertainty.

Although this event occurred years ago, I have discovered that this is a common problem in contemporary church life. Since that time, I have met numbers of dedicated, committed church members who harbor serious doubts about the reality of their salvation.

How does this happen? What contributes to a professing Christian being plagued with chronic doubt? Is it caused by faulty theology or perhaps the use of inadequate or unbiblical evangelistic methods? Does it result from a lack of proper discipleship or do some people have difficulty with assurance because of their psychological make-up? Regardless of the reason, this scenario is cause for real concern to everyone who embraces the gospel of Jesus Christ and values the eternal destiny of souls.

Some people live for years with doubt about their salvation even after doing everything they were instructed to do. They prayed a prayer, said the right words, went through the prescribed steps, but they still have little or no assurance of having been genuinely saved. Some make a new profession of faith, and they are baptized again, hoping that if they did not do everything correctly the first time, they will this time.

A few years ago, a popular evangelist preached a crusade in a large church that was part of the same local association where I served as pastor. His messages emphasized the Lordship of Jesus Christ, stressing that a person must receive Christ not only as Savior but also as Lord.

He warned that if a person had received Jesus Christ as Savior but not as Lord, then that person was not saved. As a result, a significant number of the youth in that church renewed their confession of faith, and they were baptized again. Please understand that in no way am I diminishing the importance of the Lordship of Jesus Christ. The point, however, is that salvation is more than just a formula to be adhered to or a set of steps to be followed.

For example, imagine Spurgeon deciding after he was saved that Sunday morning in the little Methodist church, "Well, I don't think I was fully aware that Jesus is Lord, therefore I need to profess faith in Christ and be baptized again." No, Spurgeon did not live with doubt about his salvation due to fear he might have left something out of a prayer or skipped a step in following a plan.

One reason Spurgeon did not have this problem was because he did not save himself. God saved him. God did the work. Salvation was not something Spurgeon did for himself or to himself. When Spurgeon, in his heart, embraced Christ by faith, the transaction was done. His sins were forgiven and Christ came into his life in an unmistakable way. You will also remember in Bunyan's allegory that as Christian came up the hill to the cross, the burden on his back fell off and rolled away. Again, that was not something Christian did to himself. Instead, it was something God did. God saved him and removed his sins from him as far as the east is from the west (Ps. 103:12).

In his interview with Nicodemus, Jesus explained the work the Holy Spirit does in saving a person. Jesus said, "The wind blows where it wishes, and you hear the sound of it, but cannot tell where it comes from and where it goes. So is everyone who is born of the Spirit" (John 3:8). The Old Testament prophet Jonah proclaimed, "Salvation is of the LORD" (Jon. 2:9). The night I was saved, the Lord did something for me. He saved me, doing a work of grace in my heart and life that only he could do.

A second point worth noting is that it is impossible to experience God's grace and be unaware of it. That does not mean that a person must have a great emotional experience when he or she is saved. However, the pattern we see in scripture is that those who have a saving encounter with Jesus Christ are aware of that encounter. Salvation is not based on emotion or feelings. Nevertheless, when a person is saved, there will be an awareness of this encounter with the living God and that he has done a work of grace in that person's life.

It is tragic for people to live for years without joy, assurance and victory because they honestly do not know for sure that they are saved. Because of this, some professing Christians adopt the attitude that no one can know for sure they have been saved because everyone, if they were willing to be honest, is just like them. Some may even come to believe there is nothing to Christianity anyway, so they turn completely away from God, the Bible and the church. Then, there are those who do not openly renounce their faith, but they have renounced it, practically speaking. Their names are still on the church roll, but they do not attend church more than once or twice a year and their "faith" has no relevancy in everyday life. You may know people who fit into each of these categories, but it is important to remember, this is not the way God intended for people to live. For anyone in this condition, be assured, there is hope. There is an answer. You can be saved and know for sure that you are.

REFLECTIONS ON CHAPTER 2

1. An ongoing pattern of serious doubts regarding one's own salvation is not God's plan nor should it be considered the norm.

2. Even those who have been genuinely saved may go through periods of experiencing doubt regarding their salvation.

3. As we continue this study, we will consider biblical guidelines for use in examining whether or not we have been saved. The result will be to clarify our relationship with the Lord and gain understanding for effective ministry to others.

AN EVANGELIST GETS SAVED

Sirs, what must I do to be saved?

— Acts 16:30

BAD COUNSEL

At the church where I had been pastor for about five years, we were in the middle of a "Revival Meeting." The visiting evangelist was Bro. Paul Ragland, who has since gone to be with the Lord. Bro. Ragland was a very godly man who was unique in many ways. One of those ways was that he served in the ministry ten years before he was saved. To some, that may seem impossible, but it is true.

His story went like this (P. Ragland, personal communication, September 1987): As a boy growing up in a small town in southern Arkansas, Paul Ragland's family attended the local Baptist church. When he was about twelve years of age, his Sunday school teacher asked everyone in the class who was a member of the church to raise his or her hand. Except for Paul and two of his friends, everyone did raise his or her hand. After the class ended, the teacher asked the boys why they were not members of the church. They replied that they just never had joined the church. The teacher responded, "Well boys, don't you think it's about time you did?" They said, "Yes Ma'am, guess it is."

That Sunday morning, Paul and his two friends walked down the aisle when the invitation was extended. They were voted into the church and were baptized that night. After the evening service, while playing on the church grounds, Paul and his friends laughed and poked fun at each other about being baptized. Bro. Ragland said that no one took the Bible and explained to them how to be saved. The attitude was that these boys had grown up in the church, most of the other kids their age had already joined the church, and so it was time for them to do the same thing, which they did.

INTO THE MINISTRY

Near the time he finished high school, Paul felt a desire to go into the ministry, so he publicly surrendered to the gospel ministry. After high school, he served in the U.S. Navy, then attended Bible college, and after that went to seminary. After completing seminary, he went into full-time evangelism, preaching in churches around the country. Being a dedicated student of God's word and believing it to be divinely inspired, Paul Ragland's preaching was Bible-centered. He had been in the ministry about ten years and was preaching a revival meeting at a church in Houston, Texas, when a dramatic event occurred in his life. During the Thursday evening service, after finishing his sermon and extending the invitation, numbers of people responded by leaving their seats and coming to the front for prayer. In fact, the altar was filled with people. Then, something completely unexpected occurred.

CONVICTION

As Paul Ragland knelt in prayer on the platform, all at once, he saw for the first time in his life that he was a sinner and that he had never been saved. He said it was as though a knife had pierced him as his eyes were opened to this awful truth. His experience was somewhat similar to those who heard the Apostle Peter preach on the Day of Pentecost. Peter boldly proclaimed, "Therefore let all the house of Israel know assuredly that God has made this Jesus, who you crucified, both Lord and Christ" (Acts 2:36). The response of the hearers is recorded in verse 37, "Now when they heard this, they were *cut to the heart*, and said to Peter and the rest of the apostles, 'Men and brethren, what shall we do?'" It is interesting that the word in the original text, which is translated "cut to the heart" (NKJV) or "pricked in their heart" (KJV) literally means "to pierce thoroughly, to agitate violently, or to sting to the quick" (Strong, 1970).

That is precisely what happened to Paul Ragland that night in Houston, Texas. Bro. Ragland said the first thought that went through his mind was, "Lord, I can't be lost. I'm a preacher," but that did not help. His next thought was, "Lord, how can I be lost? Look at all these people kneeling here in the altar." That did not help either. As quickly as possible, he ended his part of the service. Distraught and disturbed, he did not know what to do. He could not bear the thought of anyone finding out about this. What would his seminary professors think? What would his friends think if they found out he had never been saved?

Bro. Ragland became so upset that later that night, he actually went to the emergency room at a nearby hospital. They could not find anything wrong, physically. After being released, he returned to his hotel room. Throughout the night, he wrestled with God. The Holy Spirit had pierced his heart and opened his eyes, revealing to him beyond any doubt that he was lost and had never been saved. This, however, was not something he was ready to accept. If people heard about this, it would ruin him. People who were his friends would be shocked. They might even think he had become unstable or perhaps wonder if he had been a fraud all along, but he was not a fraud. He had simply never experienced God's saving grace but did not realize that until the Holy Spirit revealed it to him that night in Houston, Texas.

WHAT TO DO

As Bro. Ragland thought about what to do, he devised a plan. If he could just get out of Houston, everything would be all right. So, he decided to tell the pastor of the church that he was not feeling well and would have to leave the meeting early. After all, he had gone to the emergency room that night. He would get a flight out of Houston and would then be fine. He did not go through with his plan though. According to Bro. Ragland, God told him, not in an audible voice but just as unmistakably, that if he got on an airplane and ran, he would never knock at his heart's door again. He immediately dropped that idea.

All that night and the next day, he continued to argue with God. He knew he was lost, but he could not, or would not, accept it. The following night, which was Friday, he preached knowing he was a lost sinner. Bro. Ragland said that was the hardest thing he had ever done in his life. As soon as the service ended, he hurried back to his hotel room where Satan continued to appeal to his pride, "What will people think of you if they find out about this?" That night and the next morning, the battle continued to rage in his heart, until Saturday afternoon, when the end finally came.

SAVED AT LAST

As he got down on his hands and knees in the middle of his hotel room, Paul Ragland said that he finally waved the white flag of surrender. He told the Lord he was not willing to go to hell, no matter what anyone thought or said. He then told the Lord that he was not going to fight him, and he was not going to run from him any longer. He admitted to God that he had been right about him all along, he was just an ole sinner, and even though he was a preacher, he had never been saved.

As he knelt on his hands and knees in total submission, he asked the Lord to have mercy upon him and to save his soul. That Saturday afternoon in the privacy of his hotel room, Paul Ragland became a new creation in Christ Jesus. He finally experienced the grace of God he had been preaching about for ten years and had been professing since he was a twelve-year-old boy. As he wept and rejoiced in his newfound Savior's love, it occurred to him that he had a problem. The thought came to his mind, "I've got to preach tonight, but what am I going to say? I am the evangelist, and I just got saved." Bro. Ragland said the Holy Spirit impressed upon him that just as Nicodemus (John 3) was a lost preacher who got saved, he should simply share with the congregation what happened to him that afternoon.

During the service that night, he shared with the people how the Lord had saved his soul that afternoon. The Holy

Spirit moved upon the congregation in convicting power and by the time the revival ended the next day, over one hundred people, the majority of whom were already members of the church, had been saved. Just like the evangelist, their names were on the church roll, but they had never personally experienced God's saving grace. They had been professors, but not possessors, of eternal life.

REFLECTIONS ON CHAPTER 3

1. Some profess to know the Lord without actually knowing him (Matt. 7:21–23). A profession is valid only if it reflects genuine repentance and faith in the Lord Jesus Christ (Rom. 10: 9–10).
2. When a person experiences doubt, appealing to a past profession of faith is not sufficient to remove those doubts.
3. Church membership, dedicated service, and even ministerial success will not save a person, nor do they guarantee one has been saved.

THE TRUTH WILL MAKE YOU FREE

And you shall know the truth,
and the truth shall make you free.

— J o h n   8 : 3 2

DOUBTS ADMITTED

Our guest evangelist, Bro. Paul Ragland, concluded his sermon and extended the invitation. A woman who was a member of our congregation came forward. As she took my hand, she said, "Bro. Gary, I don't know if I am saved or not." After the closing prayer, Bro. Ragland and I went with this lady and her husband to my study. She shared with us her concern that she had been a church member for years but did not know for sure if she was saved.

Naturally, as a young pastor, I was very interested to hear how Bro. Ragland would counsel this person. I anticipated he would probably ask her to share with us when she thought she had been saved, then give her some relevant scripture dealing with assurance and, finally, pray with her. To my surprise, he did none of those things. Instead, he explained to her it was not possible for him to tell her if she had been saved and even if he could, it would do her no good because it would not satisfy her doubts. Only the Lord could satisfy those doubts and confirm to her whether or not she was saved.

He went on to explain that one of two things was happening in her life. The first possibility was that she had truly been saved but since that time had committed some sin that she had not confessed and made right with the Lord. If this was the problem, then this sin was destroying her assurance, and the Holy Spirit would not restore it until she dealt with her sin by confessing it and seeking God's forgiveness. The second possible reason for her lack of assurance, he said, was that she had never been saved. Bro. Ragland then explained that he did not know which of those two was causing the problem, but he assured her that if she genuinely wanted to know the answer and was willing to accept it, the Lord would reveal the answer to her.

If it were the first, God would reveal to her the sin which she had not dealt with and was blocking her assurance. If it were the second, God would reveal to her in an unmistakable way that she was lost and needed to be saved. He then instructed her to go home and get alone with God. He assured her again that, if she would be honest with God and was willing to accept the truth, regardless of what that was, God would reveal the answer to her.

THE HOLY SPIRIT REVEALS

About forty minutes after returning home from the service, the phone rang. It was this lady's husband. He told me that his wife needed to talk with me right away. I replied, "Meet me in my study. I will be there when you arrive." The church was approximately one mile from our house so I arrived first. About five minutes later, I heard their car in the parking lot. As they walked through the door of the study, before I could say anything, she exclaimed, "It's just like Bro. Ragland said. I had just gotten into bed when all at once, God showed me as clear as could be that I was lost and had never been saved." She insisted that she was lost and needed to be saved.

SURRENDER

After sharing a few verses of scripture with her, I asked if she would like me to lead her in a prayer. She indicated that yes, she would. In the middle of this prayer, she broke down and began weeping. She then excitedly exclaimed, "I've just been saved! I've just been saved!" She continued to cry and to laugh at the same time. Bro. Ragland arrived in just a few minutes, and we rejoiced with her and her husband that she had been born into the family of God. What a thrill as this long-time church member and dedicated worker experienced, for the first time, God's saving grace. She had heard about it, she had read about it, and she had talked about it, but she had never personally experienced salvation until that night.

In this particular case, doubt was not a bad thing. Physical pain, for example, does not feel good, but it serves a vital purpose. If your hand is touching a hot stove, pain communicates to the brain that something is wrong. One's conscience also serves a positive purpose by causing inner pain or discomfort when we violate God's law. This inner pain brings to our consciousness the realization that we have done something that is displeasing to God. When this woman experienced doubt regarding her salvation, she became aware that something was wrong in her relationship with God. The Holy Spirit caused this doubt, making her aware that not all was well. In this instance, doubt was not a negative factor. Instead, it was positive in that it made her aware that she had a spiritual need.

WISE COUNSEL

What is interesting is that Bro. Ragland counseled the dear woman that he could not tell her whether she had been saved. He told her only the Lord could do that. She was very fortunate she was not counseled by someone intent upon "convincing" her she had nothing to worry about and that her doubts were all unfounded. There was a legitimate reason for her doubts. It was because she had not been saved! Church member? Yes. Committed worker? Yes. Unfortunately, however, she had never met the Lord. She had never become a new creation in Christ Jesus. Could it be that some people have a problem with assurance because they have never been saved?

The Bible speaks about the witness of the Holy Spirit in the life of a child of God. The Apostle Paul wrote in Romans 8:16, "The Spirit Himself bears witness with our spirit that we are children of God." It is also recorded in 1 John 5:10, "He who believes in the Son of God has the witness in himself." Both of these verses refer to the inner witness of the Holy Spirit. One of the changes brought about when a person is saved is that the Holy Spirit takes up residence in that person's heart and life. The presence of the Holy Spirit is real, not imaginary. Before being saved, we were dead in trespasses and in sin and had no fellowship with God. When we are saved, we are made alive in Christ (Eph. 2:1). On the other hand, if a person has not been saved, then the Holy Spirit does not live within that person's heart, and there will be no inner witness that the individual is forgiven and is a possessor of eternal life.

For certain, when a person has doubts about his or her salvation, those doubts should not be flippantly ignored or dismissed. Instead, there should be a careful examination to determine if the concerns one is experiencing are valid. The Apostle Paul instructed those at Corinth, "Examine yourselves as to whether you are in the faith" (2 Cor. 13:5). Paul actually instructed those in the church to examine themselves to ascertain whether they were truly saved. He did not indicate that one should ignore doubts or that doubts were always misconstrued. Instead, he instructed the Corinthians to examine themselves to make sure they had been saved and were truly in the faith instead of resting upon a false hope.

Obviously, the Apostle Paul was not questioning how a person is saved. He was not questioning the fact that we are saved by God's grace, which is received by means of faith. Paul admonished the church members at Corinth to do self-examination to determine whether their faith was genuine. Was it a living faith, the kind of faith that results in being justified by God? The Bible declares in James 2:1, "Even the demons believe—and tremble!" Demons, however, are not saved. Jesus spoke one of the most sober warnings in all of scripture, and it is recorded in Matthew 7:22–23. Jesus said, "Many will say to Me in that day, 'Lord, Lord, have we not prophesied [preached] in Your name, cast out demons in Your name, and done many wonders in Your name?' And then I will declare to them, 'I never knew you; DEPART FROM ME, YOU WHO PRACTICE LAWLESSNESS.'"

In light of scripture, we should be very cautious about assuming that a person who is experiencing doubt is actually saved and has nothing about which to be concerned. As we have seen, the Holy Spirit is the one who bears witness with a person's spirit that he or she is a child of God (Rom. 8:16). God is the one who gives "the Spirit of adoption by whom we cry out, 'Abba, Father'" (Rom. 8:15), and according to the Apostle John, "He who believes in the Son of God has the witness in himself" (1 John 5:10). The Holy Spirit gives and is that inner witness.

CONCLUSIONS

Whereas we can and should share scripture with others and counsel and pray with them, only God can give a definitive answer to anyone as to whether he or she has been saved. Bro. Ragland gave wise counsel when he told this woman he could not tell her whether she had been saved, that only God could do that. But praise the Lord, God did! God did reveal to her beyond the shadow of a doubt that she was lost and needed to be saved. And, when she was saved, no one had to convince her of that. She knew God had saved her by his marvelous grace!

Dear friend, God is still working today. It is still true that salvation is of the Lord. Yes, God has commanded us to witness and to pray for the conversion of sinners, but we must also remember that we cannot convict or convert a single sinner. Only God can do that, and only God, ultimately, can give a person assurance that he or she has been saved.

REFLECTIONS ON CHAPTER 4

Do you live with persistent doubts concerning your standing with God? Have you responded by taking comfort from your profession of faith only to have those doubts persist? If you will come before the Lord with an honest desire to know the truth, he will reveal your real need. This will happen whether, as a believer, unconfessed sin has interrupted your fellowship with him or you need to come to him as a sinner, trusting him for salvation and the gift of eternal life.

HAVE YOU BEEN LOST?

> *What man of you, having a hundred sheep,*
> *if he loses one of them, does not leave the*
> *ninety-nine in the wilderness, and go after*
> *the one which is lost until he finds it? And when*
> *he has found it, he lays it on his shoulders, rejoicing.*
>
> — Luke 15:4–5

Probably, most of us have gotten turned around in the woods and experienced the feeling of being lost, at least for a brief period. Daniel Boone once quipped, "I have never been lost, but I will admit to being confused for several weeks."[1] If a person truly is lost in the great outdoors, it can prove to be an extremely traumatic and even life-threatening event.

Jesus once told the story of a shepherd who had ninety-nine sheep safe in the fold, but one sheep was missing. Knowing the one sheep was lost and would not be able to find its way back to safety, the shepherd went out searching for it. Maybe this sheep never even realized it was lost. Perhaps it was grazing, and it just slowly wandered away from the rest of the herd. In the same way, we can be lost spiritually, without even realizing it.

To be spiritually lost means that we are separated from God by sin, that we stand guilty before him and that we are in danger of eternal damnation. An extraordinarily important question then is this, "Have you been lost in a spiritual sense?" This question is critical, as we will see, because a person cannot be saved before becoming aware of and fully convinced that they are lost.

---

1. Daniel Boone, quoted in "Famous Quotes," Thinkexist. com, http://en.thinkexist.com/search/searchquotation.asp? (accessed December 29, 2008).

GARY W. DIGBY

INTO THE BIBLE

In the sixteenth chapter of the Gospel of John, Jesus was preparing his disciples for his own departure and the coming of the Comforter, the Holy Spirit. Jesus explained to them, "Nevertheless I tell you the truth. It is to your advantage that I go away; for if I do not go away, the Helper (Comforter, Holy Spirit) will not come to you; but if I depart, I will send Him to you. And when He has come, He will convict the world of sin, and of righteousness, and of judgment: of sin, because they do not believe in Me; of righteousness, because I go to My Father and you see Me no more; of judgment, because the ruler of this world is judged" (John 16:7–11).

The word *convict* (verse 8), which is translated *reprove* in the King James Version, means "to convince" or "to reveal." Jesus explained to his disciples that when the Comforter or Helper came, he would convict the world (the people of the world: men, women, boys, and girls) of three things. Those three things are the following: first, *sin* (verse 9), second, *righteousness* (verse 10), and third, *judgment* (verse 12). Thus, the Holy Spirit convicts people, reveals to them or convinces them that they are sinners, that Jesus Christ is the only source of true righteousness, and that a day of judgment is coming. Notice particularly that the first item listed that the Holy Spirit convicts people of is *sin*. One important factor that should be noted is that the word *sin* is singular, not plural. Thus, the Holy Spirit convicts people of sin, the sin of unbelief (verse 9).

Because they have not believed in the Lord Jesus Christ, they are not saved, they are not forgiven, they are not justified, they are not part of the family of God, and they are not going to heaven when they die. When the Holy Spirit brings conviction, he moves upon that person's heart and opens the eyes of his or her understanding to this spiritual reality, convincing him or her of this truth. Again, the word *sin* is singular. Therefore, when the Holy Spirit brings conviction, he does not convict people regarding their *sins*, what they have *done*, as much as he convicts them of *sin*, what they *are*. He deals with them, not about their *actions*, but about their *condition*. Before being saved, a person is lost and in danger of eternal damnation. As a result, the Holy Spirit convinces or reveals to that person his condition: that he is lost. An important principle to remember is that after a person has been saved, the Holy Spirit will never again convict that person of being lost. He will convict a saved person regarding specific acts of sin that must be confessed and forsaken in order to maintain fellowship with God, but he never convicts a child of God of being lost.

This same distinction between sin and sins is also found in the book of Romans where the Apostle Paul wrote, "All have sinned and fall short of the glory of God" (Rom. 3:23). This verse relates to what we *do*—our actions. That is, all of us have committed acts of sin. We have done deeds that transgress God's law. Paul also wrote in this same chapter, "There is none righteous, no, not one" (Rom. 3:10). Whereas verse 23 relates to our actions, verse 10 relates to what we *are*—our condition. We are unrighteous. The Bible clearly reveals that we are sinners because we sin, but it also reveals that we sin because we are sinners.

Every human being is born with a sin nature. Theologically, this is known as original sin. King David was referring to this when he wrote in Psalm 51:5, "Behold, I was brought forth in iniquity, and in sin my mother conceived me." The Apostle Paul further explained, "Therefore, just as through one man [Adam] sin entered the world, and death through sin, and thus death spread to all men, because all sinned" (Rom. 5:12). Because Adam, the first man, sinned by breaking God's command not to eat the fruit of the tree of the knowledge of good and evil, he became a sinner. Every part of his being was marred and tainted by sin. Not only did Adam become a sinner, but he also plunged the human race into sin. As a result, every descendant of Adam has been polluted by sin because the sin nature has been passed on to each of us, as well as the penalty for sin—physical and spiritual death. Thus, when a person experiences the convicting work of the Holy Spirit, the Holy Spirit deals with that person, not so much about what they have done, but about what they are—they are sinners; they are spiritually lost.

This is precisely what happened to Paul Ragland while he was kneeling in prayer in the church in Houston, Texas. This is also what happened to the woman described in the previous chapter when the Holy Spirit turned the light on in her heart, opening her eyes to see that she was lost and had never been saved. Clearly everyone is a sinner, for the Bible declares, "There is not a just man on earth who does good and does not sin" (Eccl. 7:20). The prophet Isaiah explained, "Behold, the LORD'S hand is not shortened, that it cannot save; nor His ear heavy, that it cannot hear. But your iniquities have separated you from your God; and your sins have hidden His face from you, so that He will not hear" (Is. 59:1–2). Although every person is a sinner, no one can be saved until he comes to this realization, recognizing he is lost. And, the only one who can reveal this to a person is the Holy Spirit. He does this by illuminating one's heart to this awful truth.

WHAT ABOUT CHILDREN?

Sometimes the statement is made that if a person is saved at a young age, that person will likely experience little, if any, conviction by the Holy Spirit. The idea is that a person, who has not committed many "big" sins and has not lived a wicked lifestyle, may not experience conviction because he or she is not guilty of very much sin, comparatively speaking. The problem with this premise can be demonstrated by the use of the following illustration.

Imagine, for a moment, two people. One person is a young girl eight years of age. The other person is a man fifty years of age. The young girl has grown up in a Christian home and has attended Sunday school and church all her life. She has always obeyed her parents and has been a loving and thoughtful child. On the other hand, the man who is in his fifties has gone into the very depths of sin, having committed every type of sin imaginable. Now, let's suppose the Holy Spirit begins to deal with both of these individuals, convicting each one that he or she is lost, that he or she is a sinner, and that he or she needs a savior.

Now keep in mind that both individuals are lost, both are without Christ, both possess an inherent sin nature, both have sinned and come short of the glory of God, and both are dead in trespasses and sins. My question, then, is this: If both people—the eight year-old girl and the fifty-year-old man—were to die suddenly in that spiritual condition, which one of the two would be lost forever? Which one would perish in his or her sins? Which one would spend eternity in hell? The correct answer, of course, is that if both died before coming to faith in Jesus Christ, both would be lost forever and both would suffer in a place of torment separated from God forever.

The final question then is this: Which one—the little girl or the older man—is in greater danger? The correct answer is neither one is in greater danger—BOTH are in equal danger! Before being saved, both are in grave danger because the truth is that if either one dies while lost and without Christ, he or she will face God's wrath against sin (1 Thess. 1:10) and will spend eternity in hell. Both desperately need a savior because both are dead in trespasses and in sins and need the gift of eternal life. Since this is true, it is also true that when the Holy Spirit brings conviction upon either one of them, that conviction will be real, effectual, and unmistakable. Jesus told his disciples that when the Holy Spirit had come, he would convict or convince the people of the world that they have something wrong with them—they are lost—and they need to flee to the Savior before it is too late.

In light of this, the truth is that when the young girl comes under the convicting influence of the Holy Spirit, she will experience deep and profound conviction just as will the man who has lived a life of sin. It has nothing to do with how good or bad they have been, but it has everything to do with the condition they are in—they are sinners, they are lost, they are in grave danger—and for either one to get to heaven, he or she MUST be saved by God's grace. However, before either one can be saved, he or she must first be lost. In their innermost beings, they must become aware of their true spiritual conditions before God.

The question asked at the beginning of this chapter was, "Have you been lost?" If you have been saved by God's grace, then there has been a time in your life when you experienced the convicting work of the Holy Spirit, revealing to you that you were a lost sinner who needed God's salvation. The Holy Spirit does that work prior to salvation, without which no one can come to Christ and experience his saving grace. Still, some may make the argument, "I was just a child when I professed faith in Christ and because I had never done anything wrong to speak of, I did not have a sense of being lost." Lovingly, but firmly, I would caution that no one can be saved without first becoming lost. It is a spiritual impossibility.

A PARABLE

In the Gospel of Luke (Luke 18:9–14), Jesus told a parable about two men who went up to the temple to pray. One was a Pharisee who thanked God he was not like other men. He boasted that he fasted twice a week and gave tithes of all he possessed. Sadly though, he did not realize that he was actually a pride-filled, self-righteous sinner. It evidently never occurred to him that God abhorred his boasting.

The second man Jesus talked about was a tax collector. The Jews despised tax collectors and held them in derision. They were considered the lowest of the low because they were Jews who worked for the Romans while taking advantage of the people for personal gain. However, when this man prayed, Jesus said he would not even lift up his eyes toward heaven, but beat upon his breast and cried, "God be merciful to me a sinner." Interestingly, Jesus said the tax collector, not the Pharisee, went down to his house justified.

In light of this story told by Jesus, I ask the question again: Has there been a time in your life when you, like the despised tax collector, saw yourself as a sinner before God? Or, like the Pharisee, have you never recognized yourself as being a sinner? It may come as a shock, but when a person says that he or she has never had any real sense of being lost because he or she has never really done anything bad, that is very close to the attitude expressed by the Pharisee. The Pharisee's attitude was, "God, I'm thankful I'm not a sinner like other people. God, I am thankful that I am such a good person." In some ways, that is similar to a person saying that because they were young when they made a "decision for Christ" and because they had never done anything bad, they have never had any real sense of being lost. Again, I say it lovingly, but with great concern, that such a statement, when analyzed, is very similar to the sentiment expressed by the Pharisee.

My friend, Jesus died on the cross to save sinners. In fact, Jesus said to a group of scribes and Pharisees who criticized him and his disciples for eating and drinking with tax collectors and sinners, "Those who are well have no need of a physician, but those who are sick. I have not come to call the righteous, but sinners to repentance" (Luke 5:31–32). In light of this statement made by Jesus, no one who has never seen himself as a sinner has ever met the requirement for being saved. Jesus came to save sinners only. If, in your own estimation, you have never been a sinner, that means you have never qualified for being saved.

CONCLUSIONS

The Bible is very clear that every human being is a sinner. According to God's word, everyone is in cosmic rebellion against God and, as a result, deserves death, eternal death. This is an extremely serious condition to be in and when the Holy Spirit awakens a person to this reality, regardless of age or background, it is a most sobering experience. The bottom line is that anyone who has never been awakened to their true standing before God by the Holy Spirit is still lost and separated from God. For that reason, I lovingly but solemnly affirm that, before anyone can be saved, he or she must first come to the realization that he or she is lost and in need of a savior. Therefore, once again, I ask this crucial question, "Have you been lost?"

REFLECTIONS ON CHAPTER 5

1. Regardless of age, when the Holy Spirit convicts a person, revealing to them their true standing before God, that person will be profoundly troubled.
2. We do not have the ability to convict others, including those who are close to us. Only God can do that.
3. The Holy Spirit brings conviction, but we are responsible to witness and pray faithfully for the conversion of others.

NO ONE UNDERSTANDS

> *There is none who understands;*
> *There is none who seeks after God..*
>
> —Romans 3:11

SPECIAL EMPHASIS

Everything recorded in God's word is important. However, if a text appears twice in scripture, it must be particularly important. Moreover, if a text appears three times in the Bible, it must be something God does not want us to miss because it is extraordinarily important. Romans 3:10–12 is such a passage, as these verses are also found in Psalm 14 and Psalm 53. Romans 3:11 states, "There is none who understands; There is none who seeks after God." The obvious question is, *what* does no one understand, and why does no one seek after God? The answer is that no one understands what is wrong with him or her. No one understands his or her true standing before God, that he or she is a sinner under the wrath of God. God is saying that no one understands this, not the young person, nor the hardened sinner who has defied God's law for many years. Neither understands what is wrong with him until the Holy Spirit reveals it to him and convinces him of the seriousness of his condition. No one CAN understand this until the Holy Spirit breaks through the darkness and enables him or her to perceive this spiritual reality.

A passage of scripture in the New Testament which sheds light on this issue is found in 2 Corinthians 4:3–6 (NIV): "And even if our gospel is veiled, it is veiled to those who are perishing. The god of this age has blinded the minds of unbelievers, so that they cannot see the light of the gospel of the glory of Christ, who is the image of God. For we do not preach ourselves, but Jesus Christ as Lord, and ourselves as your servants for Jesus' sake. For God, who said, 'Let light shine out of darkness,' made his light shine in our hearts to give us the light of the knowledge of the glory of God in the face of Jesus Christ."

Because the god of this age has blinded our eyes and

because we are dead in trespasses and in sin due to the fall of Adam, we cannot perceive our lost condition or the remedy. Only the Holy Spirit can do this work in an individual (John 16:7–11). Only God can open blind eyes, allowing a person to see what he or she is otherwise incapable of seeing. That is why Jesus said, "No one can come to me unless the Father who sent me draws him" (John 6:44). Before the Holy Spirit opens a sinner's eyes, that person is blind to his or her true spiritual dilemma and is incapable of coming to Christ for salvation.

In *Experiencing God*, Blackaby and King (1994) explain, "Sin has affected us so deeply that no one seeks after God on his own initiative. Therefore, if we are to have any relationship with Him or His Son, God will have to take the initiative. This is exactly what He does. God draws us to Himself" (p. 86).

WISE COUNSEL

To illustrate this point, let me share the experience of one of my cousins, whom I have been close to since youth. When Kenny was five or six years of age, he began asking his parents about what it meant to be saved. They talked with him about Jesus, explaining that he died on the cross and rose again. They also talked with him about repentance and faith. At that time, however, his parents did not detect any consciousness of sin or any evidence of conviction by the Holy Spirit. Kenny also asked them about when he could be saved and how he would know when that time had come. His parents explained to him that God would make that known to him because the Holy Spirit would begin dealing with his heart.

A few years later, when he was nine years of age, during the middle of a church service, Kenny came under deep conviction by the Holy Spirit. He became greatly troubled as the Holy Spirit revealed to him that he was lost and needed to be saved. At the conclusion of the service, he confided in his parents about what had happened. They, of course, were very concerned. They counseled him as they shared scripture and prayed with him. Kenny continued in this condition for about a week, greatly burdened and earnestly seeking the Lord for salvation.

A few days later, on Sunday afternoon, God's grace saved him. That day, my older brother Lloyd and I had planned to meet Kenny and his brother at their grandparents' house after church. We were going to play together that afternoon and then go back to church that night. However, because he feared something could happen to him, such as an accident, and because being saved was so urgent to him, Kenny did not come that afternoon. I remember being very disappointed, but when we returned to church that night, everyone was thrilled to learn that Kenny had been saved that afternoon at his home.

ASSESSMENT

When a young child begins making inquiries regarding salvation, what is the best approach to take? One possibility is to lead the child through the plan of salvation, instruct him or her to repeat a sinner's prayer, and then encourage the child to make a public profession of faith followed by baptism. The concern with following this procedure is evident when contrasted with my cousin's experience. He did not experience conviction by the Holy Spirit and the realization he was lost until he was nine years of age. Before the Holy Spirit initiated his work of conviction upon Kenny's heart, a profession of faith made by him would have been based only upon intellectual assent. Remember, no one has the ability to convict another person of sin, righteousness, and judgment. Only the Holy Spirit can do that work, and he initiates it when he chooses to do so. The Holy Spirit may initiate conviction upon one person's heart when he or she is very young. Another person may be much older when this occurs. That is under God's control, not ours.

In this particular instance, my cousin's parents could have led him to make a "decision" when he first began asking them questions. However, he did not experience the convicting work of the Holy Spirit in his heart and life until several years later when he was nine years of age. Before that occurred, Kenny knew he was a sinner, factually. He knew it mentally, but not until the Holy Spirit brought conviction upon him, did he know it experientially. Not until then, did he *experience* being lost. Before that happened, being a sinner was only terminology to him. However, when the Holy Spirit made the fact that he was a sinner and lost in sin real to him, it was then that he fled to Christ for refuge. The reality is that Kenny could not have been genuinely saved prior to when the Holy Spirit brought conviction upon him. He could have become a church member before that time, and he could have received the ordinance of baptism, but it was not possible for him to have been truly saved before experiencing the convicting work of the Holy Spirit in his heart and life.

Had Kenny been encouraged to make a profession of faith and become a member of the church when he first began questioning his parents, what would have been the result? He probably would have grown in his knowledge of the Bible and would have been a good example to his peers in the church. When he became an adult, he may have become a dedicated church member, perhaps even becoming a deacon or a pastor. Or, by contrast, he might have eventually dropped out of church because something just seemed to be missing, and there was never any real satisfaction deep within. Thankfully that did not happen. Instead, God did save Kenny that Sunday afternoon, and while he was still a teenager, the Lord called him into the gospel ministry. For many years as a pastor, evangelist, and missionary, he has been used by the Lord to help multitudes of people come to faith in Jesus Christ.

Some may have a sense that too much emphasis is being placed on emotions and feelings. It is important to recognize that this work by the Holy Spirit is not about emotions and feelings. One's emotions may be affected, but the Holy Spirit does this work of convicting, convincing, and revealing to a sinner his or her lost condition and need of a savior. An objective investigation will reveal that historical, Bible-based Christianity has consistently recognized and accepted the reality of and essential nature of the convicting work of the Holy Spirit in the conversion of sinners. Remember that Jesus said, "No one *can* come to Me unless the Father who sent Me draws him" (John 6:44). Jesus did not say no one WILL come. He said that no one CAN come. Jesus was not talking about a matter of choice. He was talking about a matter of ability. Jesus said that unless the Father draws a person to him, then that person is not capable of coming to him.

How does the Father draw people to Christ? He does this through the person and work of the Holy Spirit. This is part of the Holy Spirit's ministry. It is not the totality of his ministry but the work the Holy Spirit does in a person's life prior to conversion. This is a vital part of the Holy Spirit's ministry, and it should be emphasized again that no one but the Holy Spirit can accomplish this work in a person's life. A parent, a pastor, a teacher, an evangelist, or the most committed soul winner who ever lived cannot perform this work in a person's heart, only the Holy Spirit can do that.

Does this mean we should not witness or that it is not

important to do so? No, it does not. In God's mercy and grace, he allows us to be a part of what he is doing in the world and in people's lives. He uses us as an instrument of grace. We must always remember that he is the one doing the work, and that apart from him, we can accomplish zero. In the Great Commission, Jesus commanded us to take the Gospel to all nations, and to every creature. The Holy Spirit uses God's word, which is the sword of the Spirit (Eph. 6:17), to bring conviction. Therefore, whether through personal witnessing, through preaching, teaching, distribution of the written word, or a combination of these, the Holy Spirit uses the word to bring conviction and salvation to sinners.

The Apostle Peter wrote, "Having been born again, not of corruptible seed but incorruptible, through the *word of God* which lives and abides forever" (1 Pet. 1:23). Therefore, witnessing, as well as Bible preaching and teaching, is essential. When people hear the word of God, the Holy Spirit is able to apply the word to their minds and hearts, convincing them of its truthfulness and personal relevance.

When witnessing to a person, it is very important to be sensitive in recognizing when the Holy Spirit is at work in a person's life. We are responsible to extend the outer call as we have opportunity to share a gospel witness, but only the Holy Spirit can work inside a person's heart, extending an inner call. It is possible to rush ahead of God by pressuring a person to make a "decision" before the Holy Spirit has prepared his or her heart for genuine repentance and faith in Jesus Christ. We must be sensitive to the Holy Spirit, so God can use us to cooperate with, but never hinder or interfere with the work he is doing in a person's heart and life.

THE HOLY SPIRIT'S WORK IS PERSONAL

Another important consideration is the nature of the Holy Spirit's conviction. Is it general and universal in nature, and does a person experience it throughout his or her life prior to being saved? The statement is sometimes made that you will never witness to a person whom the Holy Spirit has not already convicted. The question must be asked, however—is this an accurate statement?

Consider Saul of Tarsus who became known as the Apostle Paul. When the Lord appeared to him outside the city of Damascus, he said to him, "It is hard for you to kick against the goads" (Acts 9:5). Evidently, the Holy Spirit had been dealing with Saul ever since the stoning of Stephen at which Saul seemed to be the person in charge. Even though Saul had tried to ignore and resist this goading by the Spirit, it was difficult. This indicates there was a specific time when the Holy Spirit began the work of conviction in Saul's heart, and it continued until his conversion on the Damascus road. This is not the description of a vague, universal conviction that Saul experienced all his life. Rather, it was specific in time and nature.

Consider also the people who heard Peter preach on the Day of Pentecost. Luke recorded this account in Acts 2:37, "Now when they heard this, they were cut to the heart…" As has already been noted, the Greek word translated *cut* or *pricked* means "to sting," "to agitate violently," or "to be stabbed." Because the Greek word *katenugesan* is a verb in the passive voice, it means the subject was acted upon. It is also significant that this word is in the *aorist* tense, meaning the action took place at a moment in time. Thus, when the people heard Peter's words, they were smitten or pierced through with conviction. Their response is recorded in verse 37, "Men and brethren, what shall we do?" The conviction that they experienced that day was not vague or general in nature; rather, it was specific in time and effect. Therefore, the Holy Spirit took the words preached by the Apostle Peter and pierced the consciousness of the listeners, revealing to them that they were sinners who were guilty before God. This was a specific work of conviction initiated by the Holy Spirit upon the consciousness of these people.

Literally thousands of examples of this work of conviction by the Holy Spirit could be cited from church history and the testimony of believers down through the ages. One account that exemplifies this can be found in *The Life and Diary of David Brainerd* (2006), a classic eighteenth-century work edited by Jonathan Edwards. Brainerd was a young man who labored as a missionary to Indians in the colonies of Connecticut, New York, and New Jersey. He recorded in his diary about preaching to many who were spiritually unconcerned and who even ridiculed the gospel message. Brainerd also recorded how the Holy Spirit awakened many of those same people to their lost condition. One such entry in his diary was dated August 8, 1745:

> A young Indian woman who I believe never knew before she had a soul nor ever thought of any such

thing, hearing that there was something strange among the Indians, came it seems to see what was the matter. In her way to the Indians she called at my lodgings, and when I told her I designed presently to preach to the Indians, laughed and seemed to mock; but went however to them. I had not proceeded far in my public discourse before she felt that she had a soul; and before I had concluded my discourse, was so convinced of her sin and misery, and so distressed with concern for her soul's salvation, that she seemed like one pierced through with a dart, and cried out incessantly. After public service was over, she lay flat on the ground praying earnestly…I hearkened to know what she said, and perceived the burden of her prayer to be, "Have mercy on me, and help me to give you my heart." (p. 284)

This is typical of many other accounts recorded in Brainerd's diary. A common factor in all of them was that the change the Holy Spirit brought upon individuals was dramatic and specific, as people were transformed from an attitude of unconcern or even skepticism to one of great distress and intense urgency upon realizing their true spiritual condition.

CONCLUSIONS

As one objectively reviews the Bible and church history, the work of the Holy Spirit in convicting those who are lost is evident from Saul of Tarsus to the jailer at Philippi, from Augustine to Luther, from Wesley to Moody, all the way up to the present day. Prior to being justified by faith, a common factor in those professing faith in Christ has been an awful realization of their true standing before God and their need of a savior. No one has ever come to Christ for salvation apart from this convicting work of the Holy Spirit. It matters not the age of the person or the person's background. All are sinners, all are depraved, and all stand guilty before a just and holy God. When the Holy Spirit turns the light on inside a person and awakens him or her to this truth, that person will be fully cognizant that he or she is lost and will be profoundly troubled. The fact is that until the Holy Spirit does this work in a person's life, making him or her aware he or she is lost, that person cannot be saved.

How does this relate to parents who are concerned about the salvation of their children? As a Christian parent, you are rightly concerned that your children come to faith in Christ and that they do so early in life. I hope that the following suggestions will be helpful and instructive:

1. First, if you have young children, pray for them daily. Ask God to touch their hearts and reveal to them their lost condition. Bring them regularly and earnestly before God's throne of grace, trusting God to do this work in his perfect timing.

2. Secondly, talk with them about the gospel and the meaning of being saved. Explain to them about sin and its penalty, the substitutionary death and resurrection of Jesus Christ. Explain terms such as repentance and faith to them. Also, share with them your own testimony of how you came to faith in Jesus Christ.

3. Last but not least, share scripture with them. Encourage and help them to memorize scripture. The Apostle Paul wrote to Timothy, his son in the ministry, "And that from childhood you have known the Holy Scriptures, which are able to make you wise for salvation through faith which is in Christ Jesus" (2 Tim. 3:15). When a

person memorizes scripture and learns God's word at a young age, the Holy Spirit will use that to help them come to a saving relationship with Jesus Christ.

4. In summary, pray for them, instruct them, and counsel them. Be careful, though, not to pressure them into making a false profession. Allow God time to work in their hearts. You want to do everything you can to help them come to faith in Christ, but you want it to be genuine and to be of God.

REFLECTIONS ON CHAPTER 6

1. No one can understand his or her true standing before God apart from the Holy Spirit working in his or her heart.

2. The Holy Spirit's work of conviction is personal, and he chooses when to initiate it, not us.

3. When sharing the gospel, we should be careful not to attempt to supplant the work of the Holy Spirit in a person's life using pressured appeals.

WITH THE HEART,
ONE BELIEVES

*That if you confess with your mouth the
Lord Jesus and believe in your heart that God has
raised Him from the dead, you will be saved.
For with the heart one believes unto righteousness,
and with the mouth confession is made unto salvation.*

—Romans 10:9–10

MARTIN LUTHER SEES
THE OPEN DOOR

One of the best-known and oft-repeated conversion testimonies in church history is that of the reformer, Martin Luther. Even though Luther was a devout monk and a professor of biblical studies, fear tormented him that he was not right with God, as described by his own words:

> I greatly longed to understand Paul's Epistle to the Romans and nothing stood in the way but that one expression, "the justice of God," because I took it to mean that justice whereby God is just and deals justly in punishing the unjust. My situation was that, although an impeccable monk, I stood before God as a sinner troubled in conscience, and I had no confidence that my merit would assuage him. Therefore I did not love a just and angry God, but rather hated and murmured against him. Yet I clung to the dear Paul and had a great yearning to know what he meant.
>
> Night and day I pondered until I saw the connection between the justice of God and the statement that "the just shall live by faith!" Then I grasped that the justice of God is that righteousness by which through grace and sheer mercy God justifies us through faith. Thereupon I felt myself to be reborn and to have gone through open doors into paradise (as cited in Bainton, 1950, p. 65).

After a long period of intense searching, Martin Luther was finally able to understand that he could only be reconciled to God through faith in the atoning work of Jesus Christ. He was able to grasp the truth that salvation can only be received as a gift. It cannot be earned. It cannot be purchased. Men, women, boys, and girls are justified by God based on grace alone, and this grace can only be received by faith alone. Since God's grace can only be received by faith, what then does it mean to have faith in Jesus Christ? It means to believe with the heart truly, as stated in the introductory scripture.

A WORD STUDY

Two words in this passage of scripture (Rom. 10:9–10) are particularly important. First, consider the word *heart*. This word can refer to a physical organ that pumps blood throughout the body, but the Apostle Paul did not have this meaning in mind. Instead, *heart* in these verses refers to the essence of who we are: the core of our being. *The Random House Dictionary* (1987) defines the heart as being, "The center of the total personality, especially with reference to intuition, feeling or emotion" (p. 882). *The MacArthur Study Bible* (1997) sheds additional light in its description of saving faith: "Saving faith consists of three elements: 1) Mental: the mind understands the gospel and the truth about Christ…, 2) Emotional: one embraces the truthfulness of those facts with sorrow over sin and joy over God's mercy and grace…, and 3) Volitional: the sinner submits his will to Christ and trusts in Him alone as the only hope of salvation (p. 1692).

Thus, for one to believe with the heart unto righteousness means that all three elements of the person are involved: the intellect, the emotions, and the will.

The second word of particular importance in this passage is the word *believe*. This word is used numerous times in scripture. As recorded in the book of Acts, the jailer at Philippi asked Paul and Silas, "Sirs, what must I do to be saved?" (Acts 16:30). Their response is recorded in verse 31, "Believe on the Lord Jesus Christ, and you will be saved, you and your household."

Also, in the eighth chapter of Acts is the story of a high-ranking government official from Ethiopia who was returning to his home from Jerusalem. As he sat in his chariot, he was reading from the book of Isaiah. Philip approached the chariot and asked, "Do you understand what you are reading?" The man responded that he could not understand, unless someone taught him. Philip then began with the passage the Ethiopian was reading, Isaiah 53, and preached Jesus to him. When they came to some water along the way, the Ethiopian asked Philip, "See, here is water. What hinders me from being baptized?" Philip responded, "If you believe with *all your heart*, you may." He affirmed to Philip, "I believe that Jesus Christ is the Son of God" (verse 37). Notice that Philip's response was that he could be baptized if he believed with all of his heart. Why this stipulation? The reason was that being baptized would have been an empty ritual without genuine faith in his heart.

What is involved in truly believing or having faith in Jesus Christ? First, faith includes believing the facts concerning the gospel. One must hear the gospel, the good news that Jesus Christ is the Son of God, that he died on a cross, shed his blood as an atonement for our sins, was buried, and rose again the third day. Paul confirmed this in the book of Romans, "So then faith comes by hearing, and hearing by the word of God" (Rom. 10:17). Earlier in this same chapter, in verse 14, Paul wrote, "How then shall they call on Him in whom they have not believed? And how shall they believe in Him of whom they have not heard?" Clearly, one must know and believe the facts of the gospel in order to be saved. However, biblical faith involves more than just believing the facts of the gospel. It includes placing one's confidence and trust, unreservedly, in Jesus Christ for the forgiveness of sin and the gift of eternal life. For example, I believe in Abraham Lincoln, even though I never met him. I believe he lived and that he was a great man and a great president. Yet, I am not personally trusting Abraham Lincoln for anything. Saving faith not only believes in Jesus Christ—that he lived and he is who the Bible says he is—but it also trusts him and him alone for the saving of one's soul.

To illustrate this further, a story that shows the contrast between trust and mere mental belief has been repeated many times over the years. A man placed an announcement in the local newspaper that the next day he was going to walk a high wire across the mighty Niagara Falls. When the announced time arrived, a large crowd had gathered to witness the daring feat. True to his word, the man successfully walked the wire over Niagara Falls. Everyone was thrilled, marveling at the skill and courage demonstrated by this man in performing such a death-defying feat. After the excited onlookers quieted, he asked, "How many of you believe I could go across the falls again, but this time, carry a man on my back?" Everyone responded with great enthusiasm. They knew he could do it because they had just witnessed with their own eyes his unparalleled display of skill and bravery. He then asked, "Who wants to be first?" Immediately, there was silence. No one said a word as each began slipping away. The obvious point of this illustration is that even though the people believed *mentally,* or *theoretically,* that the high wire artist could carry someone across Niagara Falls on his back, no one believed it enough to *trust* him with his life.

The application is that trusting Jesus Christ for salvation or believing with the heart unto righteousness is more than just believing the facts of the gospel. Rather, it means that when the Holy Spirit has convicted us, and we have come to the realization that we are sinners, separated from God and without hope, that we entrust the saving of our soul and our eternal destiny to Christ and Christ alone. We do not just believe about Jesus. Instead, we trust in him, depending and resting upon him totally and completely for time and for eternity. Jesus is our only hope. He is the only one who can save us, who can deliver us, from our terrible plight. With all our heart, with all that we are, we cast ourselves upon him. When we respond with all our heart in this manner, God will respond. God will save.

Someone may be thinking, how does one come to the place of actually resting upon Jesus and truly believing on him with all his or her heart? Perhaps a look at the Sermon on the Mount, given by Jesus and recorded in the Gospel of Matthew, will shed light on this question. Jesus began his address by giving a set of spiritual principles known as the beatitudes. The first beatitude, which is basic and foundational to those that follow, is recorded in Matthew 5:3, "Blessed are the poor in spirit, for theirs is the kingdom of heaven." The word *blessed* means "fortunate," "happy," or even "to be envied." Who are those who are blessed, according to Jesus? He said those who are *poor in spirit* are blessed. That statement seems to be somewhat ironic. We normally do not think of people who are poor in spirit as being happy or enviable. Perhaps, we need to take a closer look at what the phrase "poor in spirit" means.

The word from the Greek text that is translated *poor* in English is used to describe someone who is bankrupt, utterly destitute, or in dire poverty. A form of this same word is applied to Lazarus in Luke 16:20, 22 where he is called a beggar. *Beggar* comes from the same root word as does the word *poor*, used in Matthew 5:3. Lazarus was laid at the rich man's gate, and the dogs licked his sores. He had nothing, materially or physically. That is an apt description of the meaning of the word *poor* as used in the beatitudes.

When Jesus used the phrase *poor in spirit*, he was referring to those who are spiritually bankrupt before God. Everyone is in this condition before being saved by God's grace. However, no one is aware of being spiritually bankrupt until the Holy Spirit reveals it to him or her. Jesus was saying that those who are poor in spirit are blessed because they have seen their own sin and depravity and recognize they are helpless to please God.[2] When a person's eyes are opened to this spiritual reality, realizing they have no other place to turn but to Jesus, they are in a position to be saved. That is the reason they are blessed and are to be envied.

HELPLESS AND HOPELESS

I once read an interesting story that illustrates what it means to come to the realization that, as a sinner, we are utterly

---

2. Adrian Rogers, *The Keys to the Kingdom: The Beatitudes,* Audio cassette (Memphis: Love Worth Finding Ministries, 1992).

destitute and can do nothing to save or help save ourselves. The article contained an interview with a lifeguard concerning his work. He gave some fascinating insights into how he successfully rescues people from drowning. One insight was that a person who is drowning will often endanger the life of the rescuer as well. If the person is trying to save himself and he is in a state of panic, he can actually cause both of them to drown. Because of this potential danger, the lifeguard explained that often he will swim out to the person and get close, but not close enough for the person to touch or to grab him. Just out of reach, the lifeguard said he treads water and waits. The person in distress does not understand why the lifeguard is not trying to save him. Still, he waits patiently until the person finally wears down and quits trying to save himself. At that point, the person will quit thrashing the water and stop his frantic efforts. According to the lifeguard, when the realization of helplessness and impending doom comes over a person, he can actually see the change reflected in the person's eyes. The person then knows he is going to drown, and he can do nothing about it, *unless* the lifeguard rescues him. The lifeguard said that when he sees this change come about, at that moment he moves in, takes hold of the individual, and pulls him to safety.

The application of the story is this: Whether it is after a long struggle as it was with Martin Luther or the first time one hears the gospel, believing with the heart involves coming to the end of all dependency upon self and resting totally and completely upon the Lord Jesus Christ. You see, Jesus Christ is Lord. That means he is master; he is sovereign. And, in order to be saved, we must yield to him from the core of our being, which is our hearts. You will remember Paul Ragland doing that in his hotel room when he told God that he was not going to fight him, and he was not going to run from him any longer. That prayer was not just words. He died to self, to his perceived reputation, to everything. He surrendered unconditionally to the Lord Jesus Christ from the very core of his being and cried out to God for mercy.

Just as a person who is drowning comes to realize he can do nothing to save himself and that his life is in the hands of the lifeguard, a sinner must also come to that same realization in his heart of hearts in order to be saved. He must realize that apart from Christ, he is going to be lost forever and he can do nothing about it. He is shut up to Jesus. There is no other hope of deliverance. With this realization, the individual then looks to Jesus by faith, resting in him and trusting him and him alone to take control and rescue him from sin and condemnation. This is what Paul meant when he wrote about "believing with the heart."

The Baptist Faith and Message, a statement of faith produced by the Southern Baptist Convention, includes the following explanation regarding the subject of salvation: "Regeneration, or the new birth, is a work of God's grace whereby believers become new creatures in Christ Jesus. It is a change of heart wrought by the Holy Spirit through conviction of sin, to which the sinner responds in repentance toward God and faith in the Lord Jesus Christ" (p. 11).

Apart from the regenerating work of God, brought about by the convicting work of the Holy Spirit, there is no salvation. Praying a prayer does not automatically save a person, neither does making a public profession of faith guarantee one is saved. We are saved only because of genuine repentance toward God and faith in Jesus Christ from the heart, the very core of our being.

JOHN WESLEY TRUSTS CHRIST

John Wesley, the great English preacher and revivalist, departed England in November 1735, sailing for the colony of Georgia to do missionary work in America. On the way across the Atlantic, the ship endured five storms and the people were often fearful for their lives. After one of the worst storms, Wesley wrote in his journal:

> In the midst of the psalm wherewith their [German Moravians who were also onboard] service began, the sea broke over, split the mainsail in pieces, covered the ship, and poured in between the decks, as if the great deep had already swallowed us up. A terrible screaming began among the English. The Germans calmly sung on. I asked one of them afterwards…"was you not afraid?" He answered, "I thank God, no." "But were not your women and children afraid?" He replied mildly, "No, our women and children are not afraid to die." (as cited in Tomkins, 2003, p. 45)

Wesley, however, did not have that kind of peace and

assurance in the face of death, and it troubled him. Wesley had a conversation with August Spangenberg, the leader of the Moravians in America, while in Georgia.

> "My brother," he [Spangenberg] said, "I must first ask you one or two questions. Have you the witness within yourself? Does the Spirit of God bear witness with your spirit that you are a child of God?"
>
> Wesley was quite thrown, and he did not know what to say. Spangenberg pushed him further. "Do you know Jesus Christ?"
>
> There was a pause. "I know he is the Savior of the world," replied Wesley.
>
> "True, but do you know he has saved you?"
>
> "I hope he has died to save me."
>
> "Do you know yourself?" urged Spangenberg.
>
> "I do," Wesley said. "But," he added afterwards in his journal, "I fear they were vain words." (as cited in Tomkins, 2003, p. 48)

It should be noted that the Moravians believed assurance that one had been saved accompanied true salvation. They believed that if a person did not have the inner assurance they were a child of God, it was probably an indication that they were not saved. This, undoubtedly, is the reason Spangenberg pressed the point with Wesley as to whether or not Jesus Christ had saved him and if he knew it for sure. Clearly Wesley was uncomfortable with this line of questioning by Spangenberg.

Wesley's endeavors in Georgia did not go well as they were characterized by difficulty and disappointment. He returned to England discouraged and troubled, not only because of his unsuccessful ministry in Georgia, but because he had grave doubts about his own salvation. He later commented, "I, who went to America to convert the Indians, was never myself converted to God" (as cited in Hattersley, 2003, p. 125).

Sometime after returning to England, on Wednesday evening, May 24, 1738, Wesley attained the faith for which he had longed. Wesley wrote in his journal: "In the evening, I went very unwillingly to a society in Aldersgate Street where one was reading Luther's preface to the Epistle to the Romans. About a quarter before nine, while he was describing the change which God works in the heart through faith in Christ, I felt my heart strangely warmed. I felt I did trust in Christ, Christ alone for salvation; and an assurance was given me that he had taken away my sins, even mine, and saved me from the law of sin and death" (as cited in Winchester, 1906, p. 57).

Even though Wesley went to Georgia as a minister and missionary, he had no inner assurance that his sins were forgiven and that he was prepared to meet God. He was torn by doubt and fear until, at the Aldersgate meeting, he personally experienced the peace and assurance he had witnessed in the Moravians. It was then that Wesley believed unto righteousness and received the witness of the Spirit that he was a child of God. Wesley was a preacher, a student of the Bible and theology, and he was so devoted to the cause of Christ that he made a hazardous voyage across the Atlantic to do missionary work among the Indians in the Georgia colony. In spite of all this, he had never personally experienced salvation. Salvation is a work of God, but God had never done this work in the heart and life of John Wesley until that evening at Aldersgate. When God saved him, with it came the assurance that he was saved.

CONCLUSIONS

Dear friend, salvation is not difficult. It is not complicated, but it is a work of God, and it is by grace. It can only be received from God as a gift. However, in order to receive this great salvation, you must come to God humbly, even as a little child, trusting Christ with all your heart for the forgiveness of sin and the gift of eternal life. You then can confess Jesus Christ as your personal Lord and Savior with the assurance that he truly lives in your heart and life.

REFLECTIONS ON CHAPTER 7

1. Confessing Jesus Christ apart from faith in one's heart does not result in salvation.
2. To believe means more than just believing the facts of the gospel. It also involves trusting in or resting upon Jesus Christ for salvation.
3. When we become poor in spirit, we come to the recognition that we are spiritually bankrupt, destitute, and without hope apart from God's mercy and grace.

4. Jesus Christ is Lord. As a sinner, I must yield to him and surrender to him. He is right; I am wrong. He is able to save; I am helpless. I am totally at his mercy, and I must come to grips with that reality in my innermost being.

5. We sometimes instruct people to "come to Christ just as you are." Is this wise and biblical counsel? Yes, in the sense that we cannot bring anything to Christ that merits salvation; no, in the sense that we can come to Christ without a change of heart…without a meek and contrite spirit (see Psalm 51). Jesus said, "…anyone who will not receive the kingdom of God like a little child will never enter it" (Luke 18:17, NIV).

EPILOGUE

*When...I received the gospel to my soul's
salvation, I thought that I had never really
heard it before...But, on looking back, I am
inclined to believe that I had heard the
gospel fully preached many hundreds of times
before...and when I did hear it, the message
may not have been any more clear in itself
than it had been at former times, but the
power of the Holy Spirit was present to open
my ear, and to guide the message to my heart.*

—Spurgeon, p. 98

As we have seen, one can only be saved when being convicted and drawn by the Holy Spirit. Therefore, the commonly accepted belief that a person can "make a decision for Christ" anytime he or she chooses is not supported by scripture. In the quote above by Charles Haddon Spurgeon, it is interesting that prior to conversion, Spurgeon knew the plan of salvation. As he stated, he had heard the gospel hundreds of times. Spurgeon also knew he was a sinner—that he was lost and needed to be saved. When he was actually saved, it was because he was able to understand the gospel and the things Jesus had done for him in a way he never had before. Why this change? The only possible answer is that, as Spurgeon himself said, the Holy Spirit opened his spiritual ears and guided the message to his heart. The Holy Spirit enabled him to see through eyes of faith, Jesus dying in his place, shedding his blood as atonement for his sins. This was a supernatural, divine intervention in his life, and as a result, he was saved that day.

Even though Spurgeon had prayed and diligently sought the Lord for salvation, it had been to no avail until that snowy Sunday morning in the little Methodist church. He had prayed many prayers and had earnestly sought after God, but he was not saved! That did not occur until the Holy Spirit opened his unseeing eyes, enabling him to perceive and respond to that which he had been blind to before.

What if, prior to his actual conversion, his grandfather or some other well-meaning person had persuaded Spurgeon that he was already saved? Before being converted, Spurgeon knew the gospel mentally, and by his own admission, he had prayed many times for the Lord to save him, but he was not saved. He did not experience God's grace until the Holy Spirit enabled him to respond from his heart to the gospel message. In his case, Spurgeon knew he was not saved until he personally experienced the new birth. Could it be that some precious souls live with doubt today because they made a profession of faith without actually ever experiencing the grace of God?

We, as Christians, must recognize that we can neither initiate nor orchestrate the convicting work of the Holy Spirit. Also, we cannot actually save another person anymore than we can save ourselves. God is the ONLY one who can do that. Ultimately, we are totally dependent upon

God for results in helping people come to Christ. The realization of this fact should motivate each of us to be diligent and passionate, not only in witnessing, but also in pleading for souls before God's throne of grace.

WE MUST BE SENSITIVE TO THE HOLY SPIRIT

You will remember from chapter four the story about a woman who was saved. When I shared scripture and prayed with her, she was obviously under deep conviction by the Holy Spirit and was ready to be saved. Everyone we witness to will not be at this stage. It is also significant that I did not have to tell or try to convince her that she was saved. Instead, she told me, her husband, Bro. Ragland, and anyone else who was within hearing that God had saved her soul. She did not have to be talked into believing she was saved. She *knew* she was saved, and she could not contain the love and joy that flooded her soul.

As we share scripture and explain the way of salvation, the Holy Spirit can use that to awaken people to their lost condition and draw them to Christ. The Spirit may accomplish this work very quickly or it may be over a period of weeks, months, or even years. This calls for sensitivity and discernment on the part of the person who is witnessing. Of course, we want to see people come to Christ and receive the gift of eternal life, but for the same reason, we do not want to mislead them or to give them false hope. Again, it is important not to rush in and get ahead of what God is doing in a person's life. It is also important to remember that performing spiritual acts, such as saying a prayer or receiving believer's baptism, does not necessarily mean that a person is saved. Doing a specific religious act or ritual is not synonymous with being reconciled to God. Salvation is a work only God can perform.

THE HOLY SPIRIT CONVICTS YOUNG PEOPLE TOO

When recalling the Sunday school youth department described in chapter two, it is possible that at least some of those young people had an ongoing problem with doubt because they made a profession, and they were baptized before the Holy Spirit ever dealt with their hearts and before they experienced any real concept of being lost. This is not to say young children cannot be saved, but as already discussed, the Holy Spirit must convict or convince a person of his lost condition before he can be saved, regardless of his age.

Jonathan Edwards, who was the most prominent leader of the great awakening in the American colonies during the 1730s, recorded an interesting account of the conversion of a little girl, barely four years of age, in the book entitled *A Narrative of Many Surprising Conversions* (1972). Even Edwards, himself, seemed surprised a person so young could be genuinely saved.

The little girl's name was Phebe Bartlet. Edwards described how Phebe became distressed of soul and pleaded with God for salvation. She continued in a terrible frame of mind day by day. According to Edward's account, "She continued...earnestly crying, and taking on for some time, till at length she suddenly ceased crying, and began to smile, and presently said with a smiling countenance, 'Mother, the kingdom of heaven is come to me!' " (Edwards, 1972, p. 44). Edwards wrote that Phebe Bartlet was still living in March, 1789 [she would have been fifty-eight at that time] and that she had maintained the character of a true convert. It is clear that Jonathan Edwards and the people in the community believed that, in spite of her extremely young age, this little girl was truly converted to Christ. When reading the entire account, it is evident the Holy Spirit brought conviction upon her heart, revealing to her that she was a sinner and needed to be saved.

One may know about the gospel on an intellectual level, especially those who grow up in a Christian home and in an evangelical, Bible-believing church. Yet, knowing the gospel intellectually is not enough in and of itself. For that reason, it is important for each of us to examine ourselves to determine if we are truly in the faith, to determine if we have been born again by the Spirit of God. The Apostle Peter instructed his readers to make their calling and election sure (2 Pet. 1:10). It is true that God cannot lie, he cannot fail, and he cannot break his promises. God's faithfulness, however, does not lessen the critical need to be sure we truly are in Christ, that we are in a covenant relationship with him, and that his grace has saved us. Genuine biblical salvation is a personal encounter with the living God in which our sins are forgiven, we are clothed with the perfect righteousness of Jesus Christ, and the Spirit of God seals us until the day of redemption.

CONCLUSIONS

God has not changed nor updated the way he saves sinners. There has never been and never will be but one way of salvation, and that is through the person of Jesus Christ. The only way you can be saved is to come to Jesus as a bankrupt and helpless sinner, casting yourself totally upon Christ, realizing that apart from God's mercy and grace, you will be lost forever. Salvation is found in a person. The *written* word, the Bible, points us to the *living* word, Jesus Christ. The Apostle John wrote, "And this is the testimony: that God has given us eternal life, and this life is *in His Son*. He who has the Son has life; he who does not have the Son of God does not have life" (1 John 5:11–12).

Friend, do you know Jesus Christ? Does he live in your heart? Does the Holy Spirit bear witness with your spirit that you are his child? Can you go back to a time in your life when you knew you were a sinner and, as a result, fled to Christ for refuge? If not, then let me encourage you to get alone with God right now. Pour out your heart to him, and be completely honest with him. God has promised in his word, "And you will seek Me and find Me, when you search for Me with all your heart" (Jer. 29:13). You can be saved, and you can know for sure that you are.

REFERENCES

Bainton, Roland. 1950. *Here I Stand*. NY: Abingdon-
    Cokesbury Press.

Baptist Faith and Message, The. 2000. Southern Baptist
    Convention in Nashville, Tennessee.

Blackaby, Henry, and King, Claude. 1994. *Experiencing God*.
    Nashville, TN: Broadman and Holman Publishers.

Boone, Daniel. Quoted in "Famous Quotes," Thinkexist.com,
    http://en.thinkexist.com/search/searchquotation.asp?
    (accessed December 29, 2008).

Bunyan, John. 1928. *The Pilgrim's Progress (Tercentenary Ed.)*.
    Chicago: John C. Winston Company. (Orig. pub. 1678.)

Edwards, Jonathan. 1972. *A Narrative of Many Surprising
    Conversions*. Wilmington, DE: Sovereign Grace
    Publishers. (Orig. pub. 1832.)

Edwards, Jonathan. 2006. *The Life and Diary of David Brainerd, Missionary to the Indians (the works of Jonathan Edwards)*. Peabody, MA: Hendrickson Publishers. (Orig. pub. 1749.)

Hattersley, Roy. 2003. *The Life of John Wesley: A Brand from the Burning*. New York: Doubleday.

Hudson, Ralph. 1885. At the Cross. Retrieved on June 30, 2008, from http://www.cyberhymnal. org/htm/a/l/a/alasand.htm.

MacArthur, John. 1997. *MacArthur Study Bible*. Nashville, TN: Word Publishing.

Newton, John. 1779. Amazing Grace. Retrieved on June 20, 2008, from http://www. cyberhymnal.org/htm/a/m/a/amazing_grace.htm.

Random House Dictionary, The. 2nd ed. 1987. New York: Random House, Inc.

Rogers, Adrian. 1992. *The Keys to the Kingdom: The Beatitudes*. Audio cassette. Memphis: Love Worth Finding Ministries.

Spurgeon, Charles. 2007. *The Autobiography of Charles H. Spurgeon Vol. 1: 1834–1854*. S. Spurgeon (Ed.).

Whitefish, MT: Kessinger LLC. (Orig. pub. 1898.)

Strong, James. 1970. *The Exhaustive Concordance of the Bible* (29th printing). Madison, NJ: Broadman and Holman.

Tomkins, Stephen. 2003. *John Wesley: A Biography*. Grand Rapids, MI: William B. Eerdmans Publishing Company.

Winchester, Caleb. 1906. *The Life of John Wesley: Sometime Dean of St. Paul's A. D.* New York, NY: Macmillan Publishing Co.

APPENDIX

ASSURANCE OF SALVATION

The Apostle John wrote his first epistle with the stated purpose of explaining how a person could know that he is saved and possesses the gift of eternal life. "These things I have written to you who believe in the name of the Son of God, that you may know that you have eternal life, and that you may continue to believe in the name of the Son of God" (1 John 5:13). John obviously felt it was not only possible, but also needful, for an individual to have assurance of his salvation.

This section includes criteria to assist in determining if God's grace has saved you. This list is not comprehensive but should be helpful to anyone wanting to know that he or she is a child of God.

1. Can you go back to a time in your life when you knew that you were lost? This is very important because, as we have already seen, a person cannot be saved until he first realizes he is lost, that he is a sinner who abides under the wrath of God (John 3:36). It is the work of the Holy Spirit to impress this reality upon a person's consciousness.

2. Have you come to Christ totally yielded and completely surrendered, trusting him with all your heart for the forgiveness of your sins and the gift of eternal life?

3. When God saves a person, one of the things that happens, according to the Bible, is that the person experiences peace with God. "Therefore having been justified by faith, we have peace with God through our Lord Jesus Christ" (Rom. 5:1). The prophet Isaiah wrote, "The work of righteousness will be peace, and the effect of righteousness, quietness and assurance forever" (Isa. 32:17). "For the kingdom of God is not eating and drinking, but righteousness and peace and joy in the Holy Spirit" (Rom. 14:17). Whereas, before being saved, there is a sense of guilt and condemnation. After salvation, we have peace with God and peace

within our hearts. This has been the consistent testimony of believers down through the ages.

4. At the moment of salvation, the Holy Spirit comes to live in the newborn believer's heart and life. Several verses of scripture that reveal this truth are the following: "Now hope does not disappoint, because the love of God has been poured out in our hearts by the Holy Spirit who was given to us" (Rom. 5:5). We are also told in scripture, "And do not grieve the Holy Spirit of God, by whom you were sealed for the day of redemption" (Eph. 4:30). In his second letter to the church in Corinth, the Apostle Paul wrote, "Who also has sealed us and given us the Spirit in our hearts as a guarantee" (2 Cor. 1:22). In this verse, the word *guarantee* means earnest, pledge, or down payment. When we are saved, the Holy Spirit comes to live within us, and he is the guarantee, the pledge, or the down payment that assures us that we will receive our full inheritance, and that one day, our redemption—body, soul, and spirit—will be completed. Perhaps the fullest revelation of this truth is found in Ephesians 1:13–14, "In Him you also trusted, after you heard the word of

truth, the gospel of your salvation; in whom also, having believed, you were sealed with the Holy Spirit of promise, who is the guarantee of our inheritance until the redemption of the purchased possession, to the praise of His glory."

5. Not only does the Holy Spirit come to live within us the moment we are saved, but he also bears witness with our spirit that we are children of God. Before a person is saved, the Holy Spirit convicts that person of being lost. After a person is saved, the Holy Spirit will convict the believer of specific sins committed, but the Holy Spirit will *never* convict a saved person of being lost. Notice the following verses that relate to the inner witness of the Holy Spirit: Romans 8:15–16, "For you did not receive the spirit of bondage again to fear, but you received the Spirit of adoption by whom we cry out, 'Abba, Father.' The Spirit Himself bears witness with our spirit that we are children of God." The Apostle John wrote in 1 John 5:10–12: "He who believes in the Son of God has the witness in himself; he who does not believe God has made Him a liar, because he has not believed the testimony that God has given of His

Son. And this is the testimony: that God has given us eternal life, and this life is in His Son. He who has the Son has life; he who does not have the Son of God does not have life."

John also states in 1 John 3:24b, "And by this we know that He abides in us, by the Spirit whom He has given us." These verses are referring to the inner witness of the Holy Spirit. The Holy Spirit bears witness with our spirit or to our spirit that we are saved and that we are children of God. The Holy Spirit is that witness in that he lives inside us. Before experiencing the saving grace of God, the Holy Spirit did not live within us. Upon conversion, he comes to live in the life of the believer. Whereas we were dead in trespasses and in sin, we are now alive to God. We have been born from above, born again (John 3); we have become a partaker of divine nature. The very presence of the Holy Spirit living and abiding within us is the inner witness to which the Bible refers. If a person has not experienced God's saving grace, this inner witness will not be present and cannot be manufactured. However, if God's grace has saved a person, then the Holy Spirit lives within and is an abiding witness to the believer. The inner witness of the Holy Spirit is one of the ways we know we have been saved.

6. When we are saved, we become a new creation in Christ. This new life within us will grow and produce fruit. According to Philippians 1:6, "He who has begun a good work in you will complete it until the day of Jesus Christ." We may falter and at times stumble, but the fact remains that if a person has experienced God's saving grace, the life of Christ will manifest itself in his or her life.

7. According to John's epistle, several qualities will be present in a person's life if he or she has been saved. One characteristic is that a saved person will keep God's commandments. I John 2:3–5 states, "Now by this we know that we know Him, if we keep His commandments. He who says, 'I know Him,' and does not keep His commandments, is a liar, and the truth is not in him. But whoever keeps His word, truly the love of God is perfected in him. By this we know that we are in Him." Also, I John 2:29 states, "If you know that He is righteous, you know that everyone who practices righteousness is born of Him." This does not mean that

a person who has been saved will never sin. It does mean, however, that a person who has been saved will not live a life of sin and make a habit of sinning.

If a person can enjoy practicing sin, that is, enjoy habitual sin as a way of life, John is saying that this is evidence this person has never been saved. In the Old Testament, Lot lived in the midst of sin as he dwelt in the city of Sodom. The scripture says that Lot tormented his righteous soul from day to day by seeing and hearing their lawless deeds (2 Peter 2:8). Lot could not enjoy the sinful culture that surrounded him because he was a just man. The grace of God had changed him. Remember, the Bible is not saying that if a person has been saved, he or she will never sin. It *is* saying that if a person has been saved, then that person will not be able to live a life of habitual sin because sin will bother him or her.

The reason sin bothers a person who has been saved is because he has a new nature and that nature loves those things that God loves. A person who has been saved is a new creation in Christ; old things have passed away, and all things have become new (2 Cor. 5:17). Contrary to what some people teach, this position is not advocating that works are necessary for salvation. Instead, the Bible reveals that when a person is saved, he or she receives a new heart and a new nature. If they still love a life of sin, then that simply means they have never experienced the soul-saving, life-changing grace of God. This has nothing to do with works; rather, it is the natural result of having been saved. John is saying that one of the evidences of genuine salvation is a desire to keep God's commandments because we love him and want to do those things that please him.

8. Another evidence of having been saved is that we love other believers. 1 John 2:9–11, "He who says he is in the light, and hates his brother, is in darkness until now. He who loves his brother abides in the light, and there is no cause for stumbling in him. But he who hates his brother is in darkness and walks in darkness, and does not know where he is going, because the darkness has blinded his eyes." This same principle is explained in chapter three, "We know that we have passed from death to life, because we love the brethren. He who does not love his brother abides in death. Whoever hates his brother is a murderer, and you know that no murderer has eternal life abiding in him" (1 John 3:14–15).

Of course, Cain was the first murderer in history. He became jealous of his brother Abel and hated him in his heart, which led to murder. The love to which John refers is a divine love that becomes ours when we come to know God. "He who does not love does not know God, for God is love" (1 John 4:8). Loving one's brother is a result of having been saved. It is not something we do to try to earn salvation. John is simply saying that if we are children of God, we will love the brethren. If we do not love our brothers and sisters in Christ, it is because we are still dead in trespasses and sin and have never passed from death unto life.

Other evidences of salvation could be included. These, however, are some of the primary ones revealed in scripture. As we examine ourselves objectively by the standards laid out in God's word, we should have a good sense of whether or not we have been saved because if we have, his grace will be actively at work in our lives. Some might protest that they have been living a carnal life, and for that reason, none of these characteristics is evident. The truth is that even if a saved person has been living a carnal life, and that is possible, he is going to be miserable until he repents and gets right with God. In addition, such a person will experience God's chastening hand in his life. It is simply impossible to experience the grace of God in salvation and then be able to enjoy, over an extended period, a life of habitual sin. Anyone who can do that has never been saved. In that case, the only solution is to be honest with God and come to him humbly as a sinner seeking salvation.

If you know you have been saved, but you have not been walking in fellowship with the Lord, claim 1 John 1:9. "If we confess our sins, He is faithful and just to forgive us our sins and to cleanse us from all unrighteousness." If you will be honest about your sins, confess them to God, turn from them, and humbly seek his forgiveness, God will hear and will restore your fellowship with him. Then, your life will be a source of blessing to others and bring glory to God.

ABOUT THE AUTHOR

Born November 21, 1951, Gary Digby grew up in Fulton, Mississippi, a small town in the northeastern part of the state. After graduating from Mississippi State University with a degree in secondary education, he served as a public school teacher for several years before surrendering to the gospel ministry in June 1977. He then enrolled at Mid-America Baptist Theological Seminary in Memphis, Tennessee, where he received a Master of Divinity degree in 1981 and later, a Doctor of Ministry degree in 1991. While attending seminary, he began pastoring his first church in 1978. During the past thirty-plus years, he has served as the pastor of churches in Mississippi, Arkansas, and New York. Also, from 1991–1993, he served as Vice-President for Institutional Advancement at Central Baptist College in Conway, Arkansas. Dr. Digby and his wife, Annette, presently reside in Jefferson City, Missouri, where he serves as interim pastor for a local congregation, and Annette is employed at Lincoln University as Vice-President for Academic Affairs/Provost. They have two grown children, Jeremy and Christy, both of whom are married and reside in northwest Arkansas.